'HE FELT A DEEP PIT THE FINGER JOINT THAT LAY THERE ON THE DRESSER.'

C000050750

WILLIAM S. BURROUGHS
Born 1914, Missouri, USA
Died 1997, Kansas, USA

'The Finger' was first published in *Early Routines* in 1981.
These stories are from the collection *Interzone*, which
was first published in 1989.

WILLIAM S. BURROUGHS

The Finger

PENGUIN BOOKS

PENGUIN CLASSICS

UK | USA | Canada | Ireland | Australia
India | New Zealand | South Africa

Penguin Books is part of the Penguin Random House group
of companies whose addresses can be found at
global.penguinrandomhouse.com.

This selection first published 2018
001

Copyright © William S. Burroughs, 1989

Set in 12/15 pt Dante MT Std
Typeset by Jouve (UK), Milton Keynes
Printed in Great Britain by Clays Ltd, St Ives plc

ISBN: 978-0-241-33907-7

www.greenpenguin.co.uk

Penguin Random House is committed to a
sustainable future for our business, our readers
and our planet. This book is made from Forest
Stewardship Council® certified paper.

Contents

The Finger

Lee walked slowly up Sixth Avenue from 42nd Street, looking in pawnshop windows.

'I must do it,' he repeated to himself.

Here it was. A cutlery store. He stood there shivering, with the collar of his shabby chesterfield turned up. One button had fallen off the front of his overcoat, and the loose threads twisted in a cold wind. He moved slowly around the shopwindow and into the entrance, looking at knives and scissors and pocket microscopes and air pistols and take-down tool kits with the tools snapping or screwing into a metal handle, the whole kit folding into a small leather packet. Lee remembered getting one of these kits for Christmas when he was a child.

Finally he saw what he was looking for: poultry shears like the ones his father used to cut through the joints when he carved the turkey at Grandmother's

Thanksgiving dinners. There they were, glittering and stainless, one blade smooth and sharp, the other with teeth like a saw to hold the meat in place for cutting.

Lee went in and asked to see the shears. He opened and closed the blades, tested the edge with his thumb.

'That's stainless steel, sir. Never rusts or tarnishes.'

'How much?'

'Two dollars and seventy-nine cents plus tax.'

'Okay.'

The clerk wrapped the shears in brown paper and taped the package neatly. It seemed to Lee that the crackling paper made a deafening noise in the empty store. He paid with his last five dollars, and walked out with the shears heavy in his overcoat pocket.

He walked up Sixth Avenue, repeating: 'I must do it. I've got to do it now that I've bought the shears.' He saw a sign: *Hotel Aristo*.

There was no lobby. He walked up a flight of stairs. An old man, dingy and indistinct like a faded photograph, was standing behind a desk. Lee registered, paid one dollar in advance, and picked up a key with a heavy bronze tag.

His room opened onto a dark shaft. He turned on the light. Black stained furniture, a double bed with a thin mattress and sagging springs. Lee unwrapped the shears and held them in his hand. He put the shears down on the dresser in front of an oval mirror that turned on a pivot.

Lee walked around the room. He picked up the shears again and placed the end joint of his left little finger against the saw teeth, lower blade exactly at the knuckle. Slowly he lowered the cutting blade until it rested against the flesh of his finger. He looked in the mirror, composing his face into the supercilious mask of an eighteenth-century dandy. He took a deep breath, pressed the handle quick and hard. He felt no pain. The finger joint fell on the dresser. Lee turned his hand over and looked at the stub. Blood spurted up and hit him in the face. He felt a sudden deep pity for the finger joint that lay there on the dresser, a few drops of blood gathering around the white bone. Tears came to his eyes.

'It didn't do anything,' he said in a broken child's voice. He adjusted his face again, cleaned the blood off it with a towel, and bandaged his finger crudely, adding more gauze as the blood soaked through. In a few minutes the bleeding had stopped. Lee picked up the finger joint and put it in his vest pocket. He walked out of the hotel, tossing his key on the desk.

'I've done it,' he said to himself. Waves of euphoria swept through him as he walked down the street. He stopped in a bar and ordered a double brandy, meeting all eyes with a level, friendly stare. Goodwill flowed out of him for everyone he saw, for the whole world. A lifetime of defensive hostility had fallen from him.

Half an hour later he was sitting with his analyst on a park bench in Central Park. The analyst was trying to persuade him to go to Bellevue, and had suggested they 'go outside to talk it over'.

'Really, Bill, you're doing yourself a great disservice. When you realize what you've done you'll need psychiatric care. Your ego will be overwhelmed.'

'All I need is to have this finger sewed up. I've got a date tonight.'

'Really, Bill, I don't see how I can continue as your psychiatrist if you don't follow my advice in this matter.' The analyst's voice had become whiny, shrill, almost hysterical. Lee wasn't listening; he felt a deep trust in the doctor. The doctor would take care of him. He turned to the doctor with a little-boy smile.

4

'Why don't you fix it yourself?'

'I haven't practiced since my internship, and I don't have the necessary materials in any case. This has to be sewed up right, or it could get infected right on up the arm.'

Lee finally agreed to go to Bellevue, for medical treatment only.

At Bellevue, Lee sat on a bench, waiting while the doctor talked to somebody. The doctor came back and led Lee to another room, where an intern sewed up the finger and put on a dressing. The doctor kept urging him to allow himself to be committed; Lee was overcome by a sudden faintness. A nurse told him to put his head back. Lee felt that he must put himself entirely in the care of the doctor.

'All right,' he said. 'I'll do what you say.'

The doctor patted his arm. 'Ah, you're doing the right thing, Bill.' The doctor led him past several desks, where he signed papers.

'I'm cutting red tape by the yard,' the doctor said.

Finally Lee found himself in a dressing gown in a bare ward.

'Where is my room?' he asked a nurse.

'Your room! I don't know what bed you've been assigned to. Anyway you can't go there before eight unless you have a special order from the doctor.'

'Where is my doctor?'

'Doctor Bromfield? He isn't here now. He'll be in tomorrow morning around ten.'

'I mean Doctor Horowitz.'

'Doctor Horowitz? I don't think he's on the staff here.'

He looked around him at the bare corridors, the men walking around in bathrobes, muttering under the cold, indifferent eyes of an attendant.

Why, this is the psychopathic ward, he thought. *He put me in here and went away!*

Years later, Lee would tell the story: 'Did I ever tell you about the time I got on a Van Gogh kick and cut off the end joint of my little finger?' At this point he would hold up his left hand. 'This girl, see? She lives in the next room to me in a rooming house on Jane Street. That's in the Village. I love her and she's so stupid I can't make any impression. Night after night I lay there hearing her carry on with some man in the next room. It's tearing me all apart . . . So

I hit on this finger joint gimmick. I'll present it to her: "A trifling memento of my undying affection. I suggest you wear it around your neck in a pendant filled with formaldehyde." '

'But my analyst, the lousy bastard, shanghaied me into the nuthouse, and the finger joint was sent to Potter's Field with a death certificate, because someone might find the finger joint and the police go around looking for the rest of the body.

'If you ever have occasion to cut off a finger joint, my dear, don't consider any instrument but poultry shears. That way you're sure of cutting *through* at the joint.'

'And what about the girl?'

'Oh, by the time I got out of the nuthouse she'd gone to Chicago. I never saw her again.'

Driving Lesson

The red-light district of East St Louis is a string of wood houses along the railroad tracks: a marginal district of vacant lots, decaying billboards and cracked sidewalks where weeds grow through the cracks. Here and there you see rows of corn.

Bill and Jack were drinking in a bar on one corner of the district. They had been drinking since early afternoon, and were past the point of showing signs of drunkenness. Through the door, Bill could hear frogs croaking from pools of stagnant water in the vacant lots. Above the bar was a picture of Custer's Last Stand, distributed by courtesy of Anheuser-Busch. Bill knew the picture was valuable, like a wooden Indian. He was trying to explain this to the bartender, how an object gets rare and then valuable, the value increasing geometrically as collectors buy it up.

'Yeah,' the bartender said, 'you already told me that ten times. Anything else?' He walked to the other end of the bar and studied a *Racing Form*, writing on a slip of paper with a short indelible pencil.

Jack picked up a dollar of Bill's money off the bar. 'I want to go in one of these houses,' he said.

'All right . . . enjoy yourself.' Bill watched Jack as he walked through the swinging door.

On the way back to St Louis, Bill stopped the car.

'Want to try driving a bit?' he asked. 'After all, you'll never get anywhere sitting on your ass. I remember when I was a reporter on the *St Louis News,* my city editor sent me out to get a picture of some character committed suicide or something . . . I forget . . . Anyway, I couldn't get the picture. Some female relative came to the door and said, "It would be a mockery," and they wouldn't give me the picture.

'And next morning I went in the john and there is the city editor taking his morning crap. So he asks me: "You got that picture, Morton?" And I said, "No, I couldn't get it – at least not yet."

' "Well," he says, "you'll never get anywhere sitting on your ass."

'So I start laughing, because that's exactly what he is doing, sitting on his ass, shitting. And I'll stack that up against any biographical anecdote for tasteless stupidity.'

Jack looked at Bill blankly, and then laughed. *The plain truth is, he's bone stupid*, Bill thought. He opened the door and got out and walked around the car, through the headlights, and got in the other side. Jack slid in under the wheel, looking dubiously at the gadgets in front of him. He had only driven twice before in his life, both times in Bill's car.

'Oh, it's quite simple,' Bill said. 'You learn by doing. Could you learn to play piano by reading a book about it? Certainly not.' He suddenly took Jack's chin in his hand and, turning Jack's face, kissed him lightly on the mouth. Jack laughed, showing sharp little eyeteeth.

'I always say people have more fun than anybody,' Jack said.

Bill shuddered in the summer night. 'I suppose they do,' he said. 'Well, let's get this show on the road.'

Jack started the car with a grinding of gears. The car bucked, almost stopped, shot forward. Finally he got it in high and moving at an even speed.

'You'll never learn this way,' Bill said. 'Let's see a little speed.'

It was three o'clock in the morning. Not a car on the street, not a sound. A pocket of immobile silence.

'A little speed, Jackie.' Bill's voice was the eerie, disembodied voice of a young child. 'That thing under your foot – push it on into the floor, Jackie.'

The car gathered speed, tires humming on asphalt. There was no other sound from outside.

'We have the city all to ourselves, Jackie . . . not a car on the street. Push it all the way down . . . all the way in . . . all the way, Jackie.'

Jack's face was blank, oblivious, the beautiful mouth a little open. Bill lit a cigarette from the dashboard lighter, muttering a denunciation of car lighters and car clocks. A piece of burning tobacco fell on his thigh, and he brushed it away petulantly. He looked at Jack's face and put the cigarettes away.

The car had moved into a dream beyond contact with the lives, forces and objects of the city. They were alone, safe, floating in the summer night, a moon spinning around the world. The dashboard shone like a fireplace, lighting the two young faces: one weak and beautiful, with a beauty that would show every day that much older; the other thin, intense, reflecting unmistakably the qualities loosely covered by the word 'intellectual,' at the same time with the look of a tormented, trapped animal. The speedometer crept up . . . 50 . . . 60 . . .

'You're learning fast, Jackie. Just keep your right foot on the floor. It's quite simple, really.'

Jack swerved to avoid the metal mounds of a safety zone. The car hit a wet spot where the street had been watered and went into a long skid. There was a squealing crash of metal. Bill flew out of the car door and slid across the asphalt. He got up and ran his hands over his thin body – nothing broken. Somebody was holding his arm.

'Are you hurt, kid?'

'I don't think so.'

He remembered seeing his car hauled away by a wrecker, the front wheels off the ground. He kept asking, 'Where is Jack?' Finally he saw Jack with two cops. Jack looked dazed. There was a bruise on his forehead, standing out sharply on the white skin.

They rode in a police car to the hospital, where the doctor put a patch on Jack's forehead. He found a cut on Bill's leg, and swabbed it with Mercurochrome.

At the police station, Bill asked to call his father. It seemed to Bill literally no time before his father appeared, conjured by an alcoholic time trick. Suddenly there he was, cool and distant as always, talking to the cops. They had hit a parked car. The owner of the other car was there.

'So I met my wife at the train and took her to see the new car, and there wasn't any car. All four wheels knocked off.'

'That will all be taken care of,' Mr Morton told him.

'Well, I should think so. That car can't be fixed. There's nothing left of it.'

'In that case you will get a new car.'

'Well, I should think so! People driving like that should be in jail. Endangering people's lives!' He glared at Bill and Jack.

One of the cops looked at him coldly. 'We'll decide who to put in jail, mister. The gentleman is getting you a new car. What are you kicking about?'

'Well, so long as I get a new car.'

There was an exchange of cards and arrangements. The desk sergeant accepted one of Mr Morton's cigars and shook hands with him. No one paid any attention to the owner of the other car.

Bill and Jack walked out of the station with Mr Morton.

'Where do you want to be dropped off?' Mr Morton asked Jack. Jack told him. He got out at his street, and Bill said, 'Good night, Jack. I'll give you a ring.'

Jack said, 'Thank you, Mr Morton.' Mr Morton shifted his cigar without answering. He put the car in gear and drove away.

It was a long ride to the Mortons' house in the suburbs. Father and son rode in silence. Finally Bill said, 'I'm sorry, Dad . . . I –'

'So am I,' his father cut in.

When they reached the garage door, Bill got out and opened it, closing it again behind the car after Mr Morton got out. Mr Morton opened the door with a key in a leather folder. They entered the house in silence.

'It's all right, Mother,' Mr Morton called upstairs. 'Nobody hurt.' He started toward the pantry. 'Want some milk, Bill?'

'No, thanks, Dad.'

Bill went upstairs to bed.

The Junky's Christmas

It was Christmas Day and Danny the Car Wiper hit the street junk-sick and broke after seventy-two hours in the precinct jail. It was a clear bright day, but there was no warmth in the sun. Danny shivered with an inner cold. He turned up the collar of his worn, greasy black overcoat.

This beat benny wouldn't pawn for a deuce, he thought.

He was in the West Nineties. A long block of brownstone rooming houses. Here and there a holy wreath in a clean black window. Danny's senses registered everything sharp and clear, with the painful intensity of junk sickness. The light hurt his dilated eyes.

He walked past a car, darting his pale blue eyes sideways in quick appraisal. There was a package on the seat and one of the ventilator windows was unlocked.

Danny walked on ten feet. No one in sight. He snapped his fingers and went through a pantomime of remembering something, and wheeled around. No one.

A bad setup, he decided. *The street being empty like this, I stand out conspicuous. Gotta make it fast.*

He reached for the ventilator window. A door opened behind him. Danny whipped out a rag and began polishing the car windows. He could feel the man standing behind him.

'What're yuh doin'?'

Danny turned as if surprised. 'Just thought your car windows needed polishing, mister.'

The man had a frog face and a Deep South accent. He was wearing a camel's-hair overcoat.

'My caah don't need polishin' or nothing stole out of it neither.'

Danny slid sideways as the man grabbed for him. 'I wasn't lookin' to steal nothing, mister. I'm from the South too. Florida –'

'Goddamned sneakin' thief!'

Danny walked away fast and turned a corner.

Better get out of the neighborhood. That hick is likely to call the law.

He walked fifteen blocks. Sweat ran down his

body. There was a raw ache in his lungs. His lips drew back off his yellow teeth in a snarl of desperation.

I gotta score somehow. If I had some decent clothes . . .

Danny saw a suitcase standing in a doorway. Good leather. He stopped and pretended to look for a cigarette.

Funny, he thought. *No one around. Inside maybe, phoning for a cab.*

The corner was only a few houses away. Danny took a deep breath and picked up the suitcase. He made the corner. Another block, another corner. The case was heavy.

I got a score here all right, he thought. *Maybe enough for a sixteenth and a room.* Danny shivered and twitched, feeling a warm room and heroin emptying into his vein. *Let's have a quick look.*

He stepped into Morningside Park. No one around. *Jesus, I never see the town this empty.*

He opened the suitcase. Two long packages in brown wrapping paper. He took one out. It felt like meat. He tore the package open at one end, revealing a woman's naked foot. The toenails were painted with purple-red polish. He dropped the leg with a sneer of disgust.

'Holy Jesus!' he exclaimed. 'The routines people put down these days. Legs! Well, I got a case anyway.' He dumped the other leg out. No bloodstains. He snapped the case shut and walked away.

'Legs!' he muttered.

He found the Buyer sitting at a table in Jarrow's Cafeteria.

'Thought you might be taking the day off,' Danny said, putting the case down.

The Buyer shook his head sadly. 'I got nobody. So what's Christmas to me?' His eyes traveled over the case, poking, testing, looking for flaws. 'What was in it?'

'Nothing.'

'What's the matter? I don't pay enough?'

'I tell you there wasn't nothing in it.'

'Okay. So somebody travels with an empty suitcase. Okay.' He held up three fingers.

'For Christ's sake, Gimpy, give me a nickel.'

'You got somebody else. Why don't he give you a nickel?'

'It's like I say, the case was empty.'

Gimpy kicked at the case disparagingly. 'It's all

nicked up and kinda dirty-looking.' He sniffed suspiciously. 'How come it stink like that? Mexican leather?'

'So am I in the leather business?'

Gimpy shrugged. 'Could be.' He pulled out a roll of bills and peeled off three ones, dropping them on the table behind the napkin dispenser. 'You want?'

'Okay.' Danny picked up the money. 'You see George the Greek?' he asked.

'Where you been? He got busted two days ago.'

'Oh . . . That's bad.'

Danny walked out. *Now where can I score?* he thought. George the Greek had lasted so long, Danny thought of him as permanent. *It was good H too, and no short counts.*

Danny went up to 103rd and Broadway. Nobody in Jarrow's. Nobody in the Automat.

'Yeah,' he snarled. 'All the pushers off on the nod someplace. What they care about anybody else? So long as they get it in the vein. What they care about a sick junky?'

He wiped his nose with one finger, looking around furtively.

No use hitting those jigs in Harlem. Like as not get beat

for my money or they slip me rat poison. Might find Pan-topon Rose at Eighth and 23rd.

There was no one he knew in the 23rd Street Thompson's.

Jesus, he thought. *Where is everybody?*

He clutched his coat collar together with one hand, looking up and down the street. *There's Joey from Brooklyn. I'd know that hat anywhere.*

'Joey. Hey, Joey!'

Joey was walking away, with his back to Danny. He turned around. His face was sunken, skull-like. The gray eyes glittered under a greasy gray felt hat. Joey was sniffing at regular intervals and his eyes were watering.

No use asking him, Danny thought. They looked at each other with the hatred of disappointment.

'Guess you heard about George the Greek,' Danny said.

'Yeah. I heard. You been up to 103rd?'

'Yeah. Just came from there. Nobody around.'

'Nobody around anyplace,' Joey said. 'I can't even score for goofballs.'

'Well, Merry Christmas, Joey. See you.'

'Yeah. See you.'

*

Danny was walking fast. He had remembered a croaker on 18th Street. Of course the croaker had told him not to come back. Still, it was worth trying.

A brownstone house with a card in the window: *P. H. Zunniga, M.D.* Danny rang the bell. He heard slow steps. The door opened, and the doctor looked at Danny with bloodshot brown eyes. He was weaving slightly and supported his plump body against the doorjamb. His face was smooth, Latin, the little red mouth slack. He said nothing. He just leaned there, looking at Danny.

Goddamned alcoholic, Danny thought. He smiled.

'Merry Christmas, Doctor.'

The doctor did not reply.

'You remember me, Doctor.' Danny tried to edge past the doctor, into the house. 'I'm sorry to trouble you on Christmas Day, but I've suffered another attack.'

'Attack?'

'Yes. Facial neuralgia.' Danny twisted one side of his face into a horrible grimace. The doctor recoiled slightly, and Danny pushed into the dark hallway.

'Better shut the door or you'll be catching cold,' he said jovially, shoving the door shut.

The doctor looked at him, his eyes focusing visibly. 'I can't give you a prescription,' he said.

'But Doctor, this is a legitimate condition. An emergency, you understand.'

'No prescription. Impossible. It's against the law.'

'You took an oath, Doctor. I'm in agony.' Danny's voice shot up to a hysterical grating whine.

The doctor winced and passed a hand over his forehead.

'Let me think. I can give you one quarter-grain tablet. That's all I have in the house.'

'But, Doctor – a quarter G . . .'

The doctor stopped him. 'If your condition is legitimate, you will not need more. If it isn't, I don't want anything to do with you. Wait right here.'

The doctor weaved down the hall, leaving a wake of alcoholic breath. He came back and dropped a tablet into Danny's hand. Danny wrapped the tablet in a piece of paper and tucked it away.

'There is no charge.' The doctor put his hand on the doorknob. 'And now, my dear . . .'

'But, Doctor – can't you inject the medication?'

'No. You will obtain longer relief in using orally. Please not to return.' The doctor opened the door.

Well, this will take the edge off, and I still have money to put down on a room, Danny thought.

He knew a drugstore that sold needles without question. He bought a 26-gauge insulin needle and an eyedropper, which he selected carefully, rejecting models with a curved dropper or a thick end. Finally he bought a baby pacifier, to use instead of the bulb. He stopped in the Automat and stole a teaspoon.

Danny put down two dollars on a six-dollar-a-week room in the West Forties, where he knew the landlord. He bolted the door and put his spoon, needle and dropper on a table by the bed. He dropped the tablet in the spoon and covered it with a dropperful of water. He held a match under the spoon until the tablet dissolved. He tore a strip of paper, wet it and wrapped it around the end of the dropper, fitting the needle over the wet paper to make an airtight connection. He dropped a piece of lint from his pocket into the spoon and sucked the liquid into the dropper through the needle, holding the needle in the lint to take up the last drop.

Danny's hands trembled with excitement and his breath was quick. With a shot in front of him, his defenses gave way, and junk sickness flooded his body.

His legs began to twitch and ache. A cramp stirred in his stomach. Tears ran down his face from his smarting, burning eyes. He wrapped a handkerchief around his right arm, holding the end in his teeth. He tucked the handkerchief in, and began rubbing his arm to bring out a vein.

Guess I can hit that one, he thought, running one finger along a vein. He picked up the dropper in his left hand.

Danny heard a groan from the next room. He frowned with annoyance. Another groan. He could not help listening. He walked across the room, the dropper in his hand, and inclined his ear to the wall. The groans were coming at regular intervals, a horrible inhuman sound pushed out from the stomach.

Danny listened for a full minute. He returned to the bed and sat down. *Why don't someone call a doctor?* he thought indignantly. *It's a bringdown.* He straightened his arm and poised the needle. He tilted his head, listening again.

Oh, for Christ's sake! He tore off the handkerchief and placed the dropper in a water glass, which he hid behind the wastebasket. He stepped into the hall and knocked on the door of the next room. There was no answer. The groans continued. Danny tried the door. It was open.

The shade was up and the room was full of light. He had expected an old person somehow, but the man on the bed was very young, eighteen or twenty, fully clothed and doubled up, with his hands clasped across his stomach.

'What's wrong, kid?' Danny asked.

The boy looked at him, his eyes blank with pain. Finally he got out one word: 'Kidneys.'

'Kidney stones?' Danny smiled. 'I don't mean it's funny, kid. It's just . . . I've faked it so many times. Never saw the real thing before. I'll call an ambulance.'

The boy bit his lip. 'Won't come. Doctors won't come.' The boy hid his face in the pillow.

Danny nodded. 'They figure it's just another junky throwing a wingding for a shot. But your case is legit. Maybe if I went to the hospital and explained things . . . No, I guess that wouldn't be so good.'

'Don't live here,' the boy said, his voice muffled. 'They say I'm not entitled.'

'Yeah, I know how they are, the bureaucrat bastards. I had a friend once, died of snakebite right in the waiting room. They wouldn't even listen when he tried to explain a snake bit him. He never had enough moxie. That was fifteen years ago, down in Jacksonville . . .'

Danny trailed off. Suddenly he put out his thin, dirty hand and touched the boy's shoulder.

'I – I'm sorry, kid. You wait. I'll fix you up.'

He went back to his room and got the dropper, and returned to the boy's room.

'Roll up your sleeve, kid.' The boy fumbled his coat sleeve with a weak hand.

'That's okay. I'll get it.' Danny undid the shirt button at the wrist and pushed the shirt and coat up, baring a thin brown forearm. Danny hesitated, looking at the dropper. Sweat ran down his nose. The boy was looking up at him. Danny shoved the needle in the boy's forearm and watched the liquid drain into the flesh. He straightened up.

The boy's face began to relax. He sat up and smiled.

'Say, that stuff really works,' he said. 'You a doctor, mister?'

'No, kid.'

The boy lay down, stretching. 'I feel real sleepy. Didn't sleep all last night.' His eyes were closing.

Danny walked across the room and pulled the shade down. He went back to his room and closed the door without locking it. He sat on the bed, looking at the empty dropper. It was getting dark outside. Danny's body ached for junk, but it was a dull ache now, dull and hopeless. Numbly, he took the needle off the dropper and wrapped it in a piece of paper. Then he wrapped the needle and dropper together. He sat there with the package in his hand. *Gotta stash this someplace,* he thought.

Suddenly a warm flood pulsed through his veins and broke in his head like a thousand golden speedballs.

For Christ's sake, Danny thought. *I must have scored for the immaculate fix!*

The vegetable serenity of junk settled in his tissues. His face went slack and peaceful, and his head fell forward.

Danny the Car Wiper was on the nod.

Lee and the Boys

The sun spotlights the inner thigh of a boy sitting in shorts on a doorstep, his legs swinging open, and you fall in spasms – sperm spurting in orgasm after orgasm, grinding against the stone street, neck and back break . . . now lying dead, eyes rolled back, showing slits of white that redden slowly, as blood tears form and run down the face –

Or the sudden clean smell of salt air, piano down a city street, a dusty poplar tree shaking in the hot afternoon wind, pictures explode in the brain like skyrockets, smells, tastes, sounds shake the body, nostalgia becomes unendurable, aching pain, the brain is an overloaded switchboard sending insane messages and countermessages to the viscera. Finally the body gives up, cowering like a neurotic cat, blood pressure drops, body fluids leak through stretched, flaccid veins, shock passes to coma and death.

Somebody rapped on the outside shutter. Lee opened the shutter and looked out. An Arab boy of fourteen or so – they always look younger than they are – was standing there, smiling in a way that could only mean one thing. He said something in Spanish that Lee did not catch. Lee shook his head and started to close the shutter. The boy, still smiling, held the shutter open. Lee gave a jerk and slammed the shutter closed. He could feel the rough wood catch and tear the boy's hand. The boy turned without a word and walked away, his shoulders drooping, holding his hand. At the corner the small figure caught a patch of light.

I didn't mean to hurt him, Lee thought. He wished he had given the boy some money, a smile at least. He felt crude and detestable.

Years ago he had been riding in a hotel station wagon in the West Indies. The station wagon slowed down for a series of bumps, and a little black girl ran up smiling and threw a bouquet of flowers into the car through the rear window. A round-faced, heavy-set American in a brown gabardine suit gathered up the flowers and said, 'No want,' and tossed them at the little girl. The flowers fell in the dusty road, and the little girl turned around crying and ran away.

Lee closed the shutter slowly.

In the Rio Grande valley of South Texas, he had killed a rattlesnake with a golf club. The impact of metal on the live flesh of the snake sent an electric shiver through him.

In New York, when he was rolling lushes on the subway with Roy, at the end of the line in Brooklyn a drunk grabbed Roy and started yelling for the law. Lee hit the drunk in the face and knocked him to his knees, then kicked him in the side. A rib snapped. Lee felt a shudder of nausea.

Next day he told Roy he was through as a lush worker. Roy looked at him with his impersonal brown eyes that caught points of light, like an opal. There was a masculine gentleness in Roy's voice, a gentleness that only the strong have: 'You feel bad about kicking that mooch, don't you? You're not cut out for this sort of thing, Bill. I'll find someone else to work with.' Roy put on his hat and started to leave. He stopped with the doorknob in his hand and turned around.

'It's none of my business, Bill. But you have enough money to get by. Why don't you just quit?' He walked out without waiting for Lee to answer.

Lee did not feel like finishing the letter. He put on his coat and stepped out into the narrow, sunless street.

The druggist saw Lee standing in the doorway of the store. The store was about eight feet wide, with bottles and packages packed around three walls. The druggist smiled and held up a finger.

'One?' he said in English.

Lee nodded, looking around at the bottles and packages. The clerk handed the box of ampules to Lee without wrapping it. Lee said, 'Thank you.'

He walked away through a street lined on both sides with bazaars. Merchandise overflowed into the street, and he dodged crockery and washtubs and trays of combs and pencils and soap dishes. A train of burros loaded with charcoal blocked his way. He passed a woman with no nose, a black slit in her face, her body wrapped in grimy, padded pink cotton. Lee walked fast, twisting his body sideways, squeezing past people. He reached the sunny alleys of the outer Medina.

Walking in Tangier was like falling, plunging down dark shafts of streets, catching at corners, doorways. He passed a blind man sitting in the sun in a doorway. The man was young, with a fringe of blond beard. He sat there with one hand out, his shirt open, showing the smooth, patient flesh, the slight, immobile folds in the stomach. He sat there all day, every day.

Lee turned into his street, and a cool wind from the sea chilled the sweat on his thin body. He hooked the key into the lock and pushed the door open with his shoulder.

He tied up for the shot, and slid the needle in through a festered scab. Blood swirled up into the hypo – he was using a regular hypo these days. He pressed the plunger down with his forefinger. A passing caress of pleasure flushed through his veins. He glanced at the cheap alarm clock on the table by the bed: four o'clock. He was meeting his boy at eight. Time enough for the Eukodal to get out of his system.

Lee walked about the room. 'I have to quit,' he said over and over, feeling the gravity pull of junk in his cells. He experienced a moment of panic. A cry of despair wrenched his body: 'I have to get *out* of here. I have to make a break.'

As he said the words, he remembered whose

words they were: the Mad Dog Esposito Brothers, arrested at the scene of a multiple-slaying holdup, separated from the electric chair by a little time and a few formalities, whispered these words into a police microphone planted by their beds in the detention ward.

He sat down at the typewriter, yawned, and made some notes on a separate piece of paper. Lee often spent hours on a letter. He dropped the pencil and stared at the wall, his face blank and dreamy, reflecting on the heartwarming picture of William Lee –

He was sure the reviewers in those queer magazines like *One* would greet Willy Lee as heartwarming, except when he gets – squirming uneasily – well, you know, a bit out of line, somehow.

'Oh, that's just boyishness – after all, you know a boy's will is the wind's will, and the thoughts of youth are long, long thoughts.'

'Yes I know, but . . . the purple-assed baboons . . .'

'That's gangrened innocence.'

'Why didn't I think of *that* myself. And the piles?'

'All kids are like hung up on something.'

'So they are . . . and the prolapsed assholes feeling around, looking for a peter, like blind worms?'

'Schoolboy smut.'

'Understand, I'm not trying to *belittle* Lee –'

'You'd better not. He's a one-hundred-percent wistful boy, listening to train whistles across the winter stubble and frozen red clay of Georgia.'

– yes, there was something a trifle disquieting in the fact that the heartwarming picture of William Lee should be drawn by William Lee himself. He thought of the ultimate development in stooges, a telepathic stooge who tunes in on your psyche and says just what you want to hear: 'Boss, you is heartwarming. You is a latter-assed purple-day saint.'

Lee put down the pencil and yawned. He looked at the bed.

I'm sleepy, he decided. He took off his pants and shoes and lay down on the bed, covering himself with a cotton blanket. *They don't scratch.* He closed his eyes. Pictures streamed by, the magic lantern of junk. There is a feeling of too much junk that corresponds to the bed spinning around when you are very drunk, a feeling of gray, dead horror. The pictures in the brain are out of control, black and white, without emotion, the deadness of junk lying in the body like a viscous, thick medium.

A child came up to Lee and held up to him a bleeding hand.

'Who did this?' Lee asked. 'I'll kill him. Who did it?'

The child beckoned Lee into a dark room. He pointed at Lee with the bleeding stub of a finger. Lee woke up crying 'No! No!'

Lee looked at the clock. It was almost eight. His boy was due anytime. Lee rummaged in a drawer of the bed table and found a stick of tea. He lit it and lay back to wait for KiKi. There was a bitter, green taste in his mouth from the weed. He could feel a warm tingle spread over his body. He put his hands behind his head, stretching his ribs and arching his stomach.

Lee was forty, but he had the lean body of an adolescent. He looked down at the stomach, which curved in flat from the chest. Junk had sculpted his body down to bone and muscle. He could feel the wall of his stomach right under the skin. His skin smooth and white, he looked almost transparent, like a tropical fish, with blue veins where the hipbones protruded.

KiKi stepped in. He switched on the light.

'Sleeping?' he asked.

'No, just resting.' Lee got up and put his arms around KiKi, holding him in a long, tight embrace.

'What's the matter, Meester William?' KiKi said, laughing.

'Nothing.'

They sat down on the edge of the bed. KiKi ran his hands absently over Lee's back. He turned and looked at Lee.

'Very thin,' he said. 'You should eat more.'

Lee pulled in his stomach so it almost touched the backbone. KiKi laughed and ran his hands down Lee's ribs to the stomach. He put his thumbs on Lee's backbone and tried to encircle Lee's stomach with his hands. He got up and took off his clothes and sat down beside Lee, caressing him with casual affection.

Like many Spanish boys, KiKi did not feel love for women. To him a woman was only for sex. He had known Lee for some months, and felt a genuine fondness for him, in an offhand way. Lee was considerate and generous and did not ask KiKi to do things he didn't want to do, leaving the lovemaking on an adolescent basis. KiKi was well pleased with the arrangement.

And Lee was well pleased with KiKi. He did not like the process of looking for boys. He did not lose interest in a boy after a few contacts, not being subject to compulsive promiscuity. In Mexico he had slept with the same boy twice a week for over a year. The boy had looked enough like KiKi to be his brother. Both had very straight black hair, an Oriental look, and lean, slight bodies. Both exuded the same quality of sweet masculine innocence. Lee met the same people wherever he went.

In the Café Central

Johnny the Guide was sitting in front of the Café Central with Mrs Merrims and her sixteen-year-old son. Mrs Merrims was traveling on her husband's insurance. She was well-groomed and competent. She was making out a list of purchases and places to go. Johnny leaned forward, solicitous and deferential.

The other guides cruised by like frustrated sharks. Johnny savored their envy. His eyes slid sideways over the lean adolescent body of the boy, poised in gray flannels and a sport shirt open at the neck. Johnny licked his lips.

Hans sat several tables away. He was a German who procured boys for English and American visitors. He had a house in the native quarter – bed and boy, two dollars per night. But most of his clients went in for 'quickies.' Hans had typical Nordic features, with heavy bone structure. There was something skull-like in his face.

Morton Christie was sitting with Hans. Morton was a pathetic name-dropper and table-hopper. Hans was the only one in Tangier who could stand his silly chatter, his interminable dull lies about wealth and social prominence. One story involved two aunts, living in a house together, who hadn't spoken to each other in twenty years.

'But you see, the house is so huge that it doesn't matter, really. They each have their own set of servants and maintain completely separate households.'

Hans just sat there and smiled through all of these stories. 'It is a little girl,' he would say in defense of Morton. 'You must not be hard with him.'

Actually Morton had, through years of insecurity – sitting at tables where he wasn't wanted, desperately attempting to gain a moment's reprieve from dismissal – gained an acute sense for gossip and scandal. If someone was down with the clap, Morton always found out somehow. He had a sense for anything anyone was trying to conceal. The most perfect poker face was no protection against this telepathic penetration.

Besides, without being a good listener, sympathetic, or in any way someone you would want to confide in, he had a way of surprising confidences out of you. Sometimes you forgot he was there and said something to someone else at the table. Sometimes he would slip in a question, personal, impertinent, but you answered him before you knew it. His personality was so negative there was nothing to put you on guard. Hans found Morton's talent for collecting information useful. He could find out what was happening in town by spending half an hour listening to Morton in the Café Central.

Morton had literally no self-respect, so that his self-esteem went up or down in accordance with how others felt about him. At first he often made a good impression. He appeared naïve, boyish, friendly. Imperceptibly the naïveté degenerated into silly, mechanical chatter, his friendliness into compulsive, clinging hunger, and his boyishness faded before your eyes across a café table. You looked up and saw the deep lines about the mouth, a hard, stupid mouth like an old whore's, you saw the deep creases in the back of the neck when he craned around to look at somebody – he was always looking around restlessly, as if he were waiting for someone more important than whomever he was sitting with.

There were, to be sure, people who engaged his whole attention. He twisted in hideous convulsions of ingratiation, desperate as he saw every pitiful attempt fail flatly, often shitting in his pants with fear and excitement. Lee wondered if he went home and sobbed with despair.

Morton's attempts to please socially prominent residents and visiting celebrities, ending usually in flat failure, or a snub in the Café Central, attracted a special sort of scavenger who feeds on the humiliation and disintegration of others. These decayed queens never tired of retailing the endless saga of Morton's social failures.

'So he sat *right down* with Tennessee Williams on the beach, and Tennessee said to him: "I'm not feeling well this morning, *Michael*. I'd rather not talk to anybody." "*Michael!*" Doesn't even know his *name*! And he says, "Oh yes, Tennessee is a good friend of mine!"' And they would laugh, and throw themselves around and flip their wrists, their eyes glowing with loathsome lust.

I imagine that's the way people look when they watch someone burned at the stake, Lee thought.

At another table was a beautiful woman, of mixed Negro and Malay stock. She was delicately proportioned, with a dark, copper-colored complexion and small teeth set far apart, her nipples pointed a little upward. She was dressed in a yellow silk gown and carried herself with superb grace. At the same table sat a German woman with perfect features: golden hair curled in braids forming a tiara, a magnificent bust, and heroic proportions.

She was talking to the half-caste. When she opened her mouth to speak, she revealed horrible teeth, gray, carious, repaired rather than filled with pieces of steel – some actually rusty, others of copper covered with green verdigris. The teeth were abnormally large and crowded over each other. Broken, corroded braces stuck to them, like an old barbed-wire fence.

Ordinarily she attempted to keep her teeth covered as far as possible. However, her beautiful mouth was hardly adequate to perform this function, and the teeth peeked out here and there as she talked or ate. She never laughed if she could help it, but was subject to occasional laughing jags brought on by apparently random circumstances. The laughing jags were always followed by fits of crying, during which she would repeat over and over, 'Everybody saw my teeth! My horrible teeth!'

She was constantly saving up money to have the teeth out, but somehow she always spent the money on something else. Either she got drunk on it, or she gave it to someone in an irrational fit of generosity. She was a mark for every con artist in Tangier, because she was known to have the money she was always saving up to have her teeth out. But putting the touch on her was not without danger. She would suddenly turn vicious and maul some mooch with all the strength of her Junoesque limbs, shouting, 'You lousy bastard! Trying to con me out of my teeth money!'

Both the half-caste and the Nordic, who had taken on herself the name of Helga, were freelance whores.

Dream of the Penal Colony

That night Lee dreamed he was in a penal colony. All around were high, bare mountains. He lived in a boarding house that was never warm. He went out for a walk. As he stepped off the street corner onto a dirty cobblestone street, the cold mountain wind hit him. He tightened the belt of a leather jacket and felt the chill of final despair.

Nobody talks much after the first few years in the colony, because they know the others are in identical conditions of misery. They sit at table, eating the cold, greasy food, separate and silent as stones. Only the whiny, penetrating voice of the landlady goes on and on.

The colonists mix with the townspeople, and it is difficult to pick them out. But sooner or later they betray themselves by a misplaced intensity, which derives from the exclusive preoccupation with escape.

There is also the penal-colony look: control, without inner calm or balance; bitter knowledge, without maturity; intensity, without warmth or love.

The colonists know that any spontaneous expression of feeling brings the harshest punishment. Provocative agents continually mix with the prisoners, saying, 'Relax. Be yourself. Express your real feelings.' Lee was convinced that the means to escape lay through a relationship with one of the townspeople, and to that end he frequented the cafés.

One day he was sitting in the Metropole opposite a young man. The young man was talking about his childhood in a coastal town. Lee sat staring through the boy's head, seeing the salt marshes, the red-brick houses, the old rusty barge by the inlet where the boys took off their clothes to swim.

This may be it, Lee thought. *Easy now. Cool, cool. Don't scare him off.* Lee's stomach knotted with excitement.

During the following week, Lee tried every approach he knew, shamelessly throwing aside unsuccessful routines with a shrug: 'I was only kidding,' or, '*Son cosas de la vida.*' He descended to the most abject emotional blackmail and panhandling.

When this failed, he scaled a dangerous cliff (not quite so dangerous either, since he knew every inch of the ascent) to capture a species of beautiful green lizard found only on these ledges. He gave the boy the lizard, attached to a chain of jade.

'It took me seven years to carve that chain,' Lee said. Actually he had won the chain from a traveling salesman in a game of Latah. The boy was touched, and consented to go to bed with Lee, but soon afterward broke off intimate relationships. Lee was in despair.

I love him and besides, I haven't discovered the Secret. Perhaps he is an Agent. Lee looked at the boy with hatred. His face was breaking up, as if melted from inside by a blowtorch.

'Why won't you help me?' he demanded. 'Do you want another lizard? I will get you a black lizard with beautiful violet eyes, that lives on the west slope where the winds pick climbers from the cliff and suck them out of crevices. There is only one other purple-eyed lizard in town and that one – well, never mind. The purple-eyed lizard is more venomous than a cobra, but he never bites his master. He is the sweetest and gentlest animal on earth. Just let me show you how sweet and gentle a purple-eyed lizard can be.'

'Never mind,' said the boy, laughing. 'Anyhoo, one lizard is enough.'

'Don't say anyhoo. Well, I will cut off my foot and shrink it down by a process I learned from the Auca, and make you a watch fob.'

'What I want with your ugly old foot?'

'I will get you money for a guide and a pack train. You can return to the coast.'

'I'll go back there anytime I feel like it. My brother-in-law knows the route.'

The thought of someone being able to leave at will so enraged Lee that he was in danger of losing control. His sweaty hand gripped the snap-knife in his pocket.

The boy looked at him with distaste. 'You look very nasty. Your face has turned all sorta black, greenish-black. Are you deliberately trying to make me sick?'

Lee turned on all the control that years of confinement had taught him. His face faded from greenish-black to mahogany, and back to its normal suntanned brown color. The control was spreading through his body like a shot of M. Lee smiled smoothly, but a muscle in his cheek twitched.

'Just an old Shipibo trick. They turn themselves black for night hunting, you understand . . . Did I ever tell you about the time I ran out of K-Y in the headwaters of the Effendi? That was the year of the rindpest, when everything died, even the hyenas.'

Lee went into one of his routines. The boy was laughing now. Lee made a dinner appointment.

'All right,' said the boy. 'But no more of your Shipibo tricks.'

Lee laughed with easy joviality. 'Gave you a turn, eh, young man? Did me too, the first time I saw it. Puked up a tapeworm. Well, good night.'